To

Sloane, Colette, Brendan

"The Kid Declan"

If you ever encounter a Big
Bad Bully in your lifetime.
Please do as the book
says!!

The Chronicles of DILLON & FUZZY
Bullying Edition

Meet the Coolest Kids Ever!
– Dillon and Fuzzy!

Dillon and Fuzzy are a brother and sister duo who confront the same life adventures kids face today. In this edition, the two battle with Dillon being bullied by his friend Landus on the playground at school. Follow the journey as Dillon's teacher, along with his parents, provide valuable input on handling the meanest kid on the playground. *The Chronicles of Dillon and Fuzzy – Bullying Edition*, provides valuable life lessons and information on how to stop this vicious cycle for those who are being bullied, those who are watching the horror in silence, and those who are the unfortunate perpetrators.

NOTE FROM THE AUTHOR

If you have ever met a personable 5-year-old who greets strangers with an affectionate smile and a great big hug or handshake, you have met my amazing son Dillon. While most view his love for people as a desirable and strong trait, others may view him as being soft or weak. This, unfortunately, makes him susceptible to the bullying epidemic. Yet, when I try to emphasize the importance of protecting and standing up for himself, his reply is always, "*Yes Sir....they're my good friend and I love them.*"

Dillon sees the good in people, whatever the circumstance. I believe not only in equipping children to protect themselves from becoming victims, but also in teaching them how to keep from becoming bullies, themselves. Both aspects of this education are imperative and will ultimately provide a solid foundation to prevent bullying before it spirals out of control.

As a child I, myself, was bullied and in turn became a verbal and physical bully. My hope is that this book will help readers understand that bullying is not right and teach them how to address bullying immediately and appropriately.

This book is dedicated to Venus Hampton-Medlock, for all the times I bullied you. May this book prepare your children should they have to face any Earl B. Hunters' in their own youths.

- E.B. Hunter

Managing Editor: Tamika Hunter
Copy Editor: Ni'cola Mitchell
Illustrator: Cherie Mays
Lettering Artist: Cherie Mays
ISBN 978-0-692-52555-5

The Chronicles of

DILLON & FUZZY

Bullying Edition

Written by E. B. Hunter

Dillon, how was school today?

It was okay, I guess.....

Dillon, you know if something is bothering you, you can always talk to us, right?

Well, it's just that during playtime, Landus kicked me really hard.

Are you okay son? Did you ask him why he kicked you?

I'm okay now Dad, but it really hurt for a while. Landus is just mean, that's all. He kicks me and then walks away laughing and no one helps or says anything.

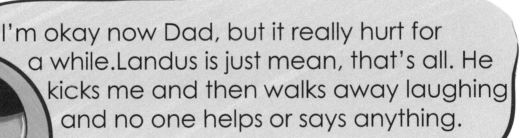

I thought you two were friends?! Has this happened before? Have you told your teacher?

Yeah Dad, Landus is mean to me a lot. Most of the time the other kids just laugh and don't help. I don't tell the teacher because I don't want to tattle.

Sometimes, Dillon, people will treat you badly because they feel bad about themselves. And others will laugh even when they want to help because that's what everyone else is doing.

Sooo....there's nothing I can do about it? He makes me so mad and I just want to hit him back!

Oh no! Fighting is never the answer, son. Tomorrow, you must tell Mrs.Collier, okay? Remember, it's not tattling if you're protecting yourself.

Dillon, why aren't you outside playing with your friends?

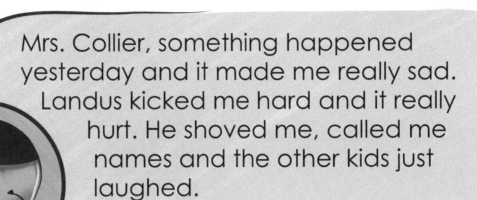

Mrs. Collier, something happened yesterday and it made me really sad. Landus kicked me hard and it really hurt. He shoved me, called me names and the other kids just laughed.

Well, that's no way for friends to treat each other. Thank you very much for telling me and trusting that I can help you. How about we go talk to Landus together right now?

Okay, if you think it will help.

Landus, have you shoved, kicked, and called Dillon names?

Yes ma'am.... I did those things to Dillon.

You two used to be friends. Why did you treat Dillon that way?

I don't like him anymore. He runs faster than me and scores better on tests, AND he never wants to play together any more.

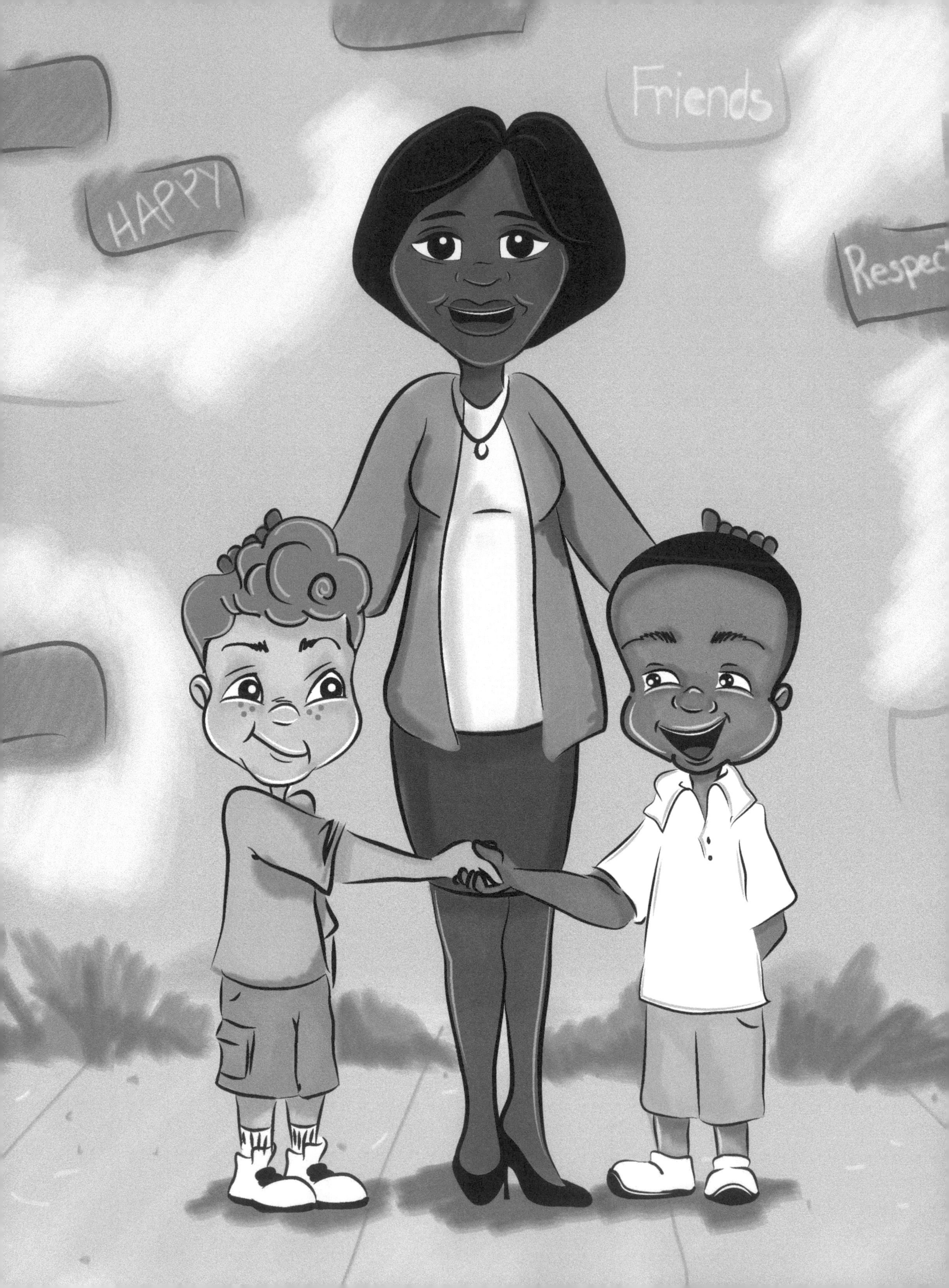
Friends
HAPPY
Respect

Landus, you cannot treat your classmates that way. Maybe Dillon doesn't want to play anymore because of how mean you are to him. You must respect your classmates at all times. And if you hurt them, you should always apologize and make up.

Dillon, I am sorry for treating you unfairly. Will you please forgive me?

Oh Landus, it's okay. I forgive you buddy, let's shake hands!

Class...I would like to talk with you about how to treat your classmates. We all know how bad bullying is, and I'm sure no one in here wants to be a bully, but I want to tell you there is something just as bad! When you see one of your classmates being bullied and you laugh at them instead of helping, you are acting just as bad as the bully. So, let's all promise each other the next time we see someone being bullied, we will all be heroes and help them by telling the teacher.

We promise Mrs. Collier!
We promise to help stop bullying!

I promise to always tell the teacher when I see someone being bullied.

I promise to never bully my classmates again!

Dillon, how was school today? Did you talk to Mrs. Collier?

School was great Dad! Yes, I talked to Mrs. Collier and she made things all better. Landus is my friend again and all the other kids promised to help if they see someone being bullied! I feel so much better!

That is AWESOME son! And now you know how to handle bullies, right?

I sure do! Whenever one of my classmates is being bullied, or if I see someone hurting or making them feel bad, I will tell an adult or teacher right away! I should never laugh when I see my friends being bullied and I certainly should never be a bully myself.

Good job Dillon! We are proud of you son!

THE END

Bullying Facts
CONFLICT RESOLUTION
from www.StopBullying.gov

Bullying is defined as "unwanted, aggressive behavior among school aged children that involves a real or perceived power imbalance. The behavior is repeated, or has the potential to be repeated, over time." It mostly takes place during or after school hours, and can occur within the school, on the playground, or on their way to and from school. Cyber bullying is aggressively taking root, as well.

The act of bullying can show in various forms, however it mainly falls into three categories:

- **Verbal** – which could include teasing, unfitting sexual comments, and name calling.

- **Relational or Social** – is intended to hurt someone's reputation or their existing and future relationships with others. These perpetrators may intentionally leave out others when playing or encourage others to not befriend the victims.

- **Physical** – involves physical contact that may include hitting, kicking, or taking items that do not belong to them.

There are many ways to prevent bullying including:

- Talk about bullying with your children. Help them understand what it means and what to do in case they are the bully, are experiencing bullying, or know someone else who is experiencing it.

- Encourage your children to take part in activities they enjoy. This will enable them to be around other children who enjoy similar interests as them.

- Be a role model for your children and their friends by always respecting others and treating them with kindness.

- Schools can get involved by putting policies in place, educating students and staff, having parents and community involvement, and creating a safe environment for students.

Dillon Hunter and Gabrielle Hunter are real life brother and sister who keep their loved ones on their toes. Dillon is a demonstrative kid who always surprises his companions with the witty things he says and does. He loves to be with his family, attend school, and play sports. He has a love for helping others and giving back to the community. Gabrielle, who is affectionately called Fuzzy by her father, is the feistier and younger one of the two. She loves her older brother and while smaller in stature, she stands up for others and always speaks her mind. The name Fuzzy comes from a great mentor who helped their dad escape the brutal cycle of bullying. Marion Cooper "Fuzzy" Thompson was instrumental in Earl's life and for this, he calls his baby girl Fuzzy.

Dillon and Fuzzy are the apple of their dad's eye and his greatest joy. He loves being a father and watching them grow and subsequently shares their latest adventures with everyone he meets. While *The Chronicles of Dillon and Fuzzy – The Bullying Edition* is the first book to be released, there are others soon to follow that deal with Dillon learning sportsmanship and Fuzzy's first day of school. Keep up to date with the latest happenings, book signings, and appearances of the dynamic duo at www. dillonandfuzzy.com.

CPSIA information can be obtained
at www.ICGtesting.com
Printed in the USA
LVHW05*1559310518
578661LV00004BA/9/P